CAIPORA : THE GUARDIAN OF THE JUNGLE

RIAN NAIR

Copyright © Rian Nair
All Rights Reserved.

This book has been published with all efforts taken to make the material error-free after the consent of the author. However, the author and the publisher do not assume and hereby disclaim any liability to any party for any loss, damage, or disruption caused by errors or omissions, whether such errors or omissions result from negligence, accident, or any other cause.

While every effort has been made to avoid any mistake or omission, this publication is being sold on the condition and understanding that neither the author nor the publishers or printers would be liable in any manner to any person by reason of any mistake or omission in this publication or for any action taken or omitted to be taken or advice rendered or accepted on the basis of this work. For any defect in printing or binding the publishers will be liable only to replace the defective copy by another copy of this work then available.

For Aran, the best little brother in existence.

Contents

Acknowledgements

Acknowledgements:

A big thanks to my parents who supported me while writing this book, especially my mom who was my personal editor! I also thank the authors Rick Riordan and Eoin Colfer, who wrote fantastic books that inspired me to write a book of my own. And of course, the biggest thanks of all to my little brother, who gave me some amazing ideas while writing this book! And last but not least my amazing uncle who made publishing this book possible!

Prologue

It was night in the Amazon rainforest. Not a sound could be heard nor could any animals be seen, except of course the serpents slithering across the trees and the scurrying of the nocturnal creatures of the jungle. But somewhere deep in a distant part of the forest, the sound of drums could be heard. In a clearing stood fifty Guarani warriors,wearing headdresses of emerald and silver feathers. Each warrior had a spear in hand and wore armour made of leather and the skins of jaguars.

They all stood in a circle around a huge stone sculpture. The walls around them were covered with banners emblazoned with an emerald serpent entwined around a gold Jaguar. The sculpture in the centre was also that of a jaguar with a serpent entwined around its neck. The Guarani chief wearing a headdress of gold and green feathers held an emerald in his hands.

"Is it time chief?" asked a soldier, who might have been the general; he spoke in his indigenous language.

"Yes," said the chief with a look of utmost certainty upon his face. He stepped up to the sculpture and placed the emerald in the serpent's mouth.

"Are you sure it will be safe here chief?" asked the general, "Many a sinful soul may approach to prise it from within its guardian. It has happened before."

"Yes," answered the chief, "But I can be confident that this time, nothing will happen. It is safeguarded. The obstacles set by you are sure to keep it safe. The Spirit of the jungle will protect the Amazon and stay a secret forever."

CHAPTER ONE

A 21st Century Morning

Sunlight streamed into the room as Gary's mother drew the curtains of his room. "Wake up Kiddo!" shouted his mom, "You've got school today."

Gary pulled aside his blanket and groaned "Uhh...I hate middle school...But I do like extra sleep!"

"You don't have a choice son," grinned his mother, "Believe me I know."

He ambled down the stairs and entered the kitchen. Gary Rodriguez was a thirteen year old boy from Brazil. He was tall and lanky with flaming red hair and long legs. Elizabeth, his mother was Irish and she too had red hair. His father, Pedro Rodriguez, however was from Rio and had jet black long hair and was very tall. Today he lounged on his favourite chair reading the newspaper and drinking a fresh cup of Brazilian coffee. Gary also had a little brother called Carlos, who was about seven years old.

Gary went to Caldone Middle School of Rio. In fact, that was where he was headed today.

"Morning Dad," said Gary.

"Hey Gary," smiled his Dad, "Good to see you up and running. I think there's something in the paper today that might interest you."

He held up the newspaper. It had a big poster of a jade relic. "Guarani sculpture," grinned his dad, "They discovered it in a lost shrine just yesterday!"

"Cool!" said Gary, "I'll check out the article after school today!"

Gary and his father loved to discuss about the indigenous culture of Brazil. His father told him many stories about the tribes of the rainforest and the creatures that roamed the jungle.

Gary gobbled his cereal and oranges, rushed up to bathe, strapped on his backpack and left for school. He reached just in time to catch the schools bright green and yellow bus and got in. He immediately spotted his two best friends, Cody and Lila Corcovado, in the backseat. Cody and Lila were twins though they didn't exactly look alike. Or so they tried to make it seem. Cody was a boy with wavy jet black hair, green eyes and was seldom seen without his headset and I-phone. Lila had hair streaked in pretty much every colour of the rainbow. Her eyes were sapphire blue and she liked to dress funky. Today she wore a green Minecraft hoodie.

"Hey Gary!!" wavedLila, a wide grin on her face. Cody however just waved his hand with eyes glued to his screen.

"What's up?" asked Gary.

"Oh, the usual," said Cody, "Lila is still an annoying person and I'm the normal one."

"Oh shut up!" said Lila, punching him playfully.

The bus suddenly pulled to a stop. They had reached Caldone Middle School.

The three of them got down. The school was a huge white building with Wooden panels above the entrance way and had big French windows, which Gary thought made it look rather like an office. The school was supposed to be one of the best in all of Rio, but Gary didn't think so. Like most children of his age, he didn't enjoy going to school. As they walked down the hallway on their way to class, a gruff voice said "Well look who it is!"

Gary stopped in his tracks. He knew that voice, but did not want to hear it.

"Giller," he muttered "what do you want?"

Giller was a tall, bulky boy with platinum blond hair and almost always wore a sneer upon his face. His real name was Giller Thomson but most of the school called him Giller the Griller. "What do I want?"sneered Giller.

"Yeah, what does a bloke like you want from me?" retorted Gary.

"You'll pay for that slick Rodriguez!" Said Giller and he punched Gary on the face.

"Dude, one day you're going to get yourself killed!" said Cody as he helped him up.

"You have got to ignore bullies like Giller, okay?" said Lila.

"Yeah," said Gary.

Their first class of the day was history. Gary didn't like history class as he felt it was the most boring class ever. The class room was a large room with rows of wooden desks and in front of them was the teachers table. Behind the table a huge blackboard was mounted onto the wall. The history classroom walls were covered with bulletin boards with charts on timelines of history, information on old forts and more. Today however, there was a new chart up on the wall. It said 'The history and Culture of Brazilian Tribes'. This came as a surprise to Gary as they hardly learned about their indigenous culture! His father had often told him about the two main tribes in Brazil, the Guarani and the Yanomami. The Guarani had supposedly died out about 100 years ago....but the Yanomami still lived in the Amazon. Just then, their teacher entered.He was a short, square shouldered man with a mop of grey hair and a moustache rather like a toothbrush! He had grey eyes which matched with his cardigan. When outside class, Gary often saw him wear what he recognized as a French beret.

"Alright class, today were going to learn about the ethnography of Brazil!" said their history teacher, Mr. Reginald Geraldo, "You all do know what that is, right?"

"I do sir!" yelled Cody, "I do! It's the study of animal behaviour!"

"Wrong!" said Geraldo, not looking too surprised, "That's *Ethology*...Does anyone else know?"

"I do," said Gary, "It's the study of tribal cultures!"

"Correct!" said Geraldo, smiling, "I expected the right answer from you Gareth!"

"Geek," sniggered Giller from the backseat.

Their teacher explained to them, all about the Amazon rainforest and the indigenous Guarani and Yanomami tribes. He told them how the rainforest looked like, how to navigate through it, which animals to watch out for and which tribes lived there.

"I suppose all of you read the newspaper today?" said Geraldo, "Today they discovered a sculpture of a Guarani deity! A miniature one for sure...but it was precious! Do any of you know what creature's sculpture it was?"

"Geraldo's face?" whispered Giller to his friend.

"That's detention for you Thompson," said Geraldo, "It was a Caipora! Can anyone tell me what that is?" Gary's hand shot up. "It was the Guarani guardian of the jungle," said Gary, "It was sometimes depicted as a Jaguar with a snakes tail and macaw wings or as a dark skinned man riding a hog. It was said to protect the animals from hunters and poachers."

"Correct," smiled Geraldo and went on with the lesson.

When the bell rang, Gary was rather disappointed as he had enjoyed that history class! Soon he and his friends had finished all the other classes and now it was lunch break. As the trio walked over to their usual spot in the cafeteria, they talked about the history class.

"That was really interesting, wasn't it?" said Lila with a grin upon her face.

"Oh, yeah it was super!" answered Gary, "What's the next period?"

"Well there's Physics with Mrs. Sanchez after Phys Ed with Mr. Galliano," said Cody, "Then we have Math with Ms. Sara and..."

"I think we get the Idea Cody," said Lila. Soon their classes had got over and had their lunch break.

"What's on the menu today?" asked Gary.

The school cafeteria was a wide room with wooden tables and benches spread out in the room. From the left of the entrance was a counter where students queued up to get their lunch. The lunch for the day was usually written on a whiteboard mounted on the right of the counter. "Well the board says its roast chicken and succotash," replied Cody.

"Oh no," grumbled Gary. If there was something Gary didn't like, it was succotash. He hated the concoction of lima beans, sweet corn and potatoes.

"Come get your grub!" yelled out Gunther de Toro, the cafeteria server. He was a short, portly, jovial man with a red handlebar moustache and spectacles.

They collected their plates of chicken and succotash and went to find a table. In one corner sat a group of girls who were giggling every five minutes for no apparent reason. On the other end, Gary saw Giller and his gang of bullies laughing about some poor kid they had probably taunted that day. Gary decided that it would be a good idea to steer clear from that table. Finally, they settled down at a table and began to eat.

"Ugh, this should be banned!" groaned Gary holding up a spoon of the mushy succotash.

"Just eat it bro," said Cody, shoving spoonfuls of it in his mouth.

Soon they had finished and were spending the rest of the lunch break roaming about. That's when Lila spotted something. "Hey, what's that?" Gary bent down and picked it up. It was a ring. A gold ring with an emerald set in it. The ring was in the shape of two entwined serpents and the emerald had ridges carved into it.

"I wonder who'd bring a ring like that to school?" asked Gary, holding it up.

"Well whoever brought it must be rich!" said Cody. "That ring must cost a million!"

Gary noticed it was rather dusty.

"Hmm...Maybe we should wash it? There might be some clue about who owns it when the dust is gone," said Gary

"Yeah," answered Lila. "That's a good idea."

The three of them rushed to the cafeteria sink. The cafeteria was empty as probably everyone had left to complete the classes for the day. They placed the ring under the tap. As soon as the drops of water touched the ring, it started to glow, the ridges emitting golden light!

"Uh, what's happening?" asked Cody, a look of fear upon his face. Suddenly they all began to glow, Gary felt as if he was being squeezed through a narrow pipe! Their visions turned hazy, their knees buckled and then they got sucked into the ring.

CHAPTER TWO

The Colonel's Cabin

Gary's vision went hazy for a moment and then it became clear. He was lying sprawled on his back on a moist surface. As he got up, he registered his surroundings. He was in a clearing of trees with thick undergrowth and dense vegetation. There were creepers and a vine hanging across the trees and the surface he was standing on was mossy and covered with grass. He felt his stomach jolt. There was only one place he had read and heard about that fit this description, but he did not want to think about it. That's when he noticed that Lila and Cody were missing.

"Lila!! Cody!!" he called out to them.

"We're here Gary!" said the distinct voice of a girl that had to be Lila. He rushed to where the voice came from. There stood Lila and Cody both frantically looking around at their surroundings.

"Gary?" said Lila looking worried, "are you thinking what I'm thinking?"

"Yes," answered Gary, "this is no Brazilian woodland. This is the Amazon Rainforest."

"Yeah, nice joke Gary," said Cody trying to look calm, though his face was as white as milk. "You're kidding right? This is just some dudes overgrown backyard?"

"Nope," replied Gary. "This has to be the rainforest. Mr.

Geraldo described it just like this."

"Well, then we're all doomed," said Cody, with a tone of finality in his voice.

"Use your I-Phone you dunce!" shouted Lila, "We can contact someone."

"Oh yeah," said Cody. He reached into his pocket and drew out a red I-Phone 11 and began to type frantically. After a few moments he groaned, "Oh no! Oh no! Oh no! Oh no!"

"What happened!" asked Lila looking terrified. "There's no signal in here!" said Cody.

"Then we're definitely doomed!" said Gary, now panic stricken.

"Who knows what will happen to us! Our parents will be worried when we don't come back home! They're going to be searching everywhere for us....but definitely not in the Amazon! Next thing we know, Acid squirting spiders are probably going to be coming after us!!" wailed Cody.

"Whoa, chill Cody!" said Lila. "First of all we're not all going to die, okay! Secondly there are no such things as Acid squirting Spiders!"

"Oh yeah!" replied Cody."Then what are those things behind you guys!" Gary and Lila turned around. He wished he hadn't. There were millions of spiders the size of crabs scuttling towards them menacingly and they were squirting liquid from their fangs that definitely looked like acid!

"Oh great, what are we going to do now?" asked Gary. Lila reached in her bag. She drew two rulers and an umbrella out of her bag.

"Why do you have that in your bag?" asked Gary bewildered.

"Oh, you never know," replied Lila, "I keep the umbrella for emergencies like now. The umbrella can be dangerous if you use it right."

Gary had no idea how the umbrella could be a lethal weapon, but he grabbed a ruler and began to swing it at the spiders. Lila was using the umbrella like a shield to fend off the spiders. Cody however was poking the spiders with his ruler as if he wanted to make them kebabs. Just when it seemed that they were going to be dinner for spiders, the sound of a roaring engine filled the air. Suddenly, a huge black jeep rode into view. The man inside shouted, "Get in!! Fast!"

The three of them pulled open the jeep's side door and scrambled in. The driver pressed down on the accelerator and they drove away, leaving the spiders behind in a cloud of dust. The man driving them had dirty blonde hair and a small wispy goatee. He wore an army jacket and his hair was tied back in a ponytail.

"Hi!" said Lila. "Thanks for saving us! But what's your name?"

The man had a deep, silky voice. "I'm Fernandez, Colonel Fernandez. And what are your names?"

"I'm Gareth Rodriguez," replied Gary "these are my best friends Lila and Cody Corcovado."

"Glad to have met you!" said Fernandez. "Come on now I'll drive you to my cabin. How did you end up in the Amazon anyway?"

"Well, you're never going to believe this, but we found this strange gold ring with a green stone in it and when we washed it, it sucked us here!" answered Cody. The colonel's face went as pale as cream cheese.

"You look a bit pale colonel?" asked Gary.

"Yes, I will explain how you got here once we reach my house." The colonel drove them down the bumpy dirt path until they came to a halt at a cabin. It was a log cabin with small windows. Torches lit up a path to the doorway with a plaque reading 'Colonel Abraxo Fernandez'. The colonel produced a key from the side pocket of his army jacket and thrust it in the rusty key hole. The four of them entered. The inside of the cabin was beautifully decorated with tribal masks and paintings. On some ledges were various exotic plants. Scarlet flames flickered in the fireplace. The colonel disappeared into the kitchen to fix them dinner. Soon he came out and placed a few dishes on the table. There were plates of freshly baked whole wheat bread, potato salad, fresh cheese and Gary's favourite, steaming chicken tamales! They all sat down and ate like a ravenous pack of wolves!

"Thanks so much!" said Gary, his mouth full of tortilla and steamed chicken. "Now, could you please tell us how we got here?"

"Of course," said Fernandez, "the reason you were brought here when you washed the ring is because that ring is an ancient Guarani relic containing a piece of a sacred stone, which supposedly held the spirit of the jungle, also known as the Caipora."

CHAPTER THREE

Quest for the Caipora

Gary choked on a piece of potato salad. "Then what was it doing in our school? And why did it bring us here when we washed it?" "The Guarani believed water to be the most powerful element, so naturally it brought you here. The ring only contains a fragment of the true Caipora stone. I don't know how it ended up in your school though," answered Colonel Fernandez. "Uh...but you can take us home right?" asked Cody.

"Sadly, No. I would definitely be willing to, but the ancient Guarani manuscripts state that the one who finds and offers the ring water, will get transported into the jungle and cannot leave until the ring is united with the true stone. Even if I tried, you would not be able to cross the boundaries of the forest.

"Oh, then we just have to find this stone and unite the ring with it," said Cody sounding relieved.

"Yes but the certain stone in question has been reputedly lost for centuries according to Fernandez," replied Lila, "If the explorers and Spanish conquistadors couldn't find it, how can we? Besides, this is sounding an awful lot like a Jumanji movie."

"But we have to try," said Gary, "speaking of which, who has the ring?"

"I have it right here," answered Lila holding up the ring.

"So it's settled then?" asked the colonel. "Tomorrow you'll leave to find the Caipora's stone."

"Yeah," answered Gary, "but will you come with us?"

"I'm afraid I can't," said the colonel, "I have forest guard duty with some other men, but I will definitely give you supplies." They all got up, said goodnight, and went to their bedrooms.

They were sleeping in Fernandez's guest room with two bunk beds. Lila and Cody were in one, Gary in the other.

"It seems like a strange coincidence that right after they find a Caipora artefact, we have to find one," said Gary, "Doesn't it?"

"It sure is...You think we'll ever get back home?" asked Lila from her top bunk, with Cody's snores in the background.

"Yeah I really think we might," answered Gary. Lila flicked the switch and the lights went out.

The next day, after a shower and a quick breakfast of avocado spread on toast, Gary and his friends got ready to leave. Fernandez generously provided them each with a backpack containing lots of food, a huge flask of water, a map of the rainforest drawn by Fernandez himself, torches, a portable tent and a special kind of headband with a torchlight on it, for exploring caves. The three of them said their goodbyes and left. They trudged through the dense rainforest following the map the colonel had given them. They weren't attacked by any animal on the way except for when a brightly coloured macaw took a great liking to Lila's rainbow coloured hair and dropped a few 'surprises' on her head. Soon Lila was muttering words as colourful as the macaw. They set up their portable tents on a small piece of bare land under a tree, surrounded by tall grassy reeds.

"This place is perfect!" grinned Cody. "We probably won't

be seen by any animal through those tall reeds!"
Soon it became night and Gary offered to keep watch while the other two slept. Gary settled himself on a rock near the fire they had made (with great difficulty) and held a branch firmly in his hands, determined not to fall asleep. After a few minutes, Gary felt extremely tired but he refused to doze off. Suddenly, he heard a whistling sound break the silence of the night! He felt a dart pierce his neck and then, he fell unconscious!

CHAPTER FOUR

Modern Magic

When Gary came to, he saw that he was tied up! Cody and Lila were tied up too, looking very surprised. But the biggest surprise was that there was a circle of people surrounding them! There were seven of them. Each person wore a loincloth and had heavily tattooed bodies. They were glaring at them, holding bows and arrows pointing right at the three of them. And they did not look happy. "What are we going to do?" asked Lila. "Who are these people anyway?" Gary remembered that in history class, Mr. Geraldo had described the Yanomami tribals exactly like the people surrounding them right now! "I think these are the Yanomami!" answered Gary. At the sound of the name of their tribe, the men surrounding them muttered something in a language Gary had never heard of! "How do we communicate with them?" asked Lila. Cody however, had a plan. "I have a language translator in my phone. I can sync it to my headset and then I can speak and understand Yanomaman!" Cody shuffled his hand into his back pocket and began to type frantically. "I've memorized the location of every app on my phone!" said Cody proudly. "Of course you have," said Lila sarcastically, "you're glued to that screen twenty-four bar seven! But seriously it actually translates Yanomaman?"

"No," shrugged Cody, "But it has a language close enough. Prepare yourselves for a long conversation in gibberish."
Soon Cody's headset light glowed blue and he spoke to one of the tribal's in their language. "*Wagatiago mana e lo fagari?*" said Cody, which must have meant, "Why have you tied up my friends and I?" The warrior muttered something back to Cody and Cody turned white. "He says we've trespassed on the tribe's territory! Apparently he blow piped you Gary with a dart coated with a poison that makes one fall asleep!" "So that's what I felt hit my neck last night!" said Gary. The tribal, still glaring at them said something. "*Takalahacha, shudobracka kapaiya!*"
At this all seven of them grinned and started jumping up and down like children given all the candy in the world. Cody's face went white again. "He says he wants to cut off our heads and then shrink and impale them on sticks!"
Gary also went white. So did Lila.
"I don't fancy becoming a shrunken head!" said Lila.
"Me neither," agreed Gary.
Then the tribal who must have been the chief said, "*Ubagagnio....*"
"That means unless!" said Cody excited, "We have a chance!"
Once again the chief spoke, "Ubagagnio, tudopamanamohigioku Shaman!"

Cody's face fell. "He will let us go free only if we can beat the head sorcerer of his tribe in magic!"

That's when Gary had the most brilliant Idea! "Hey Cody, tell him yes!" said Gary. Cody looked puzzled but still told the chief, "*Yeega!*" which probably meant yes. The chief had them put onto a wooden platform, as they were tied up and ordered for them to be carried to the village.

"You better have a plan," muttered Cody. Soon they reached a clearing full of thatched roof huts, which must have been the village. The Yanomami untied them and told them to get ready for the contest of magic. When they gathered together, closely watched by two muscular tribal's, Gary told them his plan. "Listen guys,the Yanomami don't know about electricity and other modern appliances, so I have a plan for our magic...." Soon enough they came up to the chief grinning. The chief summoned the sorcerer of the village. He was a tall hook nosed man, with long dreadlocks. He wore the skin of a snake and he held a huge staff.

Gary and his friends walked up. The sorcerer took his position in front of them.

"Ready?" exhaled Gary.

"Yep," sighed Cody," I never thought I would ever be doing this. A magic contest in a jungle, honestly."

"Just shut up," said Lila, "So we can get over with this."

The sorcerer went first. He threw a strange powder at the grass and it erupted in fire! Then he held up a branch from the fire that was burnt and black, which he covered in a cloth and brought out a new and un-burnt branch! Then he did a strange dance around the fire and it disappeared! Now it was their turn. Gary tapped his forehead and a ray of light shot out of it. Gary new perfectly well that it was the headband light Fernandez had given him, but the Yanomami thought light had erupted from his forehead! Then Lila brought her umbrella out. She had just opened it up, but the Yanomami thought she had conjured a branch into a big shield! The Grand finale was Cody though. He tapped his phone and Cody's favourite hard rock song filled the air. The Yanomami were screaming, holding their ears. As for Cody, he just danced!

"*Maga togoshakana!!*" shrieked the chief.

"He wants us to make it stop!" said Cody grinning.

"Let's not!" yelled Gary over the music.

"*Shakana! Shakana! Padurana ma Sheraka!*"

"Let's show them some mercy shall we?" grinned Lila.

Cody sighed and tapped his phone and the music stopped.

"*Tudo Vacta! Tudo Vacta!*" shrieked the chief. "It means we won!" said Cody happily.

"Great!" said Lila. The three of them asked the chief if he knew anything about the location of the Caipora. The chief did not know, but he did know someone who did! "Haga Nama Camila! Ala Oguda Guarani!" spoke the chief.

"This person's name is Camilia apparently," said Cody. "No Lila, not Camila Cabello!! He says that she lives on the farthest bank down the Amazon River. She is supposedly the last living Guarani!" "Great!" said Gary, "Then we have to go meet her!" The three of them left the village immediately to find her. They finally reached the Amazon River. It was a huge raging river, the water lashing against the river bank. "No wonder they call this the largest river in the world," said Lila, awestruck. "Yeah, I feel sorry for anyone who has to cross this river!" said Cody. "Well, too bad. We are going to be crossing this river," said Gary, "I have a plan. I remember my cousin Pauligo from Murro Sao Paulo. When I went there for the holidays, we used to go boating at a lake. He taught me how to make a raft from reeds and wood! Maybe we can make one like that!" "Yeah, that's a great idea!" said Lila. "What do you think Cody?" asked Gary. But Cody seemed to be in his own dream world, muttering something about never getting to play Fortnite again. "Alright, I'll get the wood, there are plenty of logs scattered around from last night's rain," said Gary. "Lila, you and Cody gather lots of reeds and anything strong to tie up the wood." Soon they had gathered all the supplies they needed. Suddenly Cody arrived shouting and holding something up. "Just look at this! The perfect rope," yelled Cody. He was holding a really thick, scaly kind of rope. When he arrived, he shouted, "This is a perfect rope!" Lila seemed to recognize what it actually was though, as she was shouting at him to put in down. When he came closer though, Gary froze in horror. Cody had brought a Boa Constrictor to them thinking it was rope! What a dunderhead! And now it had wrapped itself around his neck! Lila ran towards Cody with her umbrella. She squeezed her umbrella between the snake and Cody's neck to pry the snake off. Few minutes later Cody was free, Lila was panting and the snake was slithering away with the air of an animal that had just lost its meal. Gary rushed to Cody to see if he was alright. Lila was scolding Cody, when he arrived. "And next time, don't bring a Boa Constrictor as a rope!" shouted Lila, holding up her umbrella menacingly. "Whoa, I'm glad you're safe Cody!" said Gary relieved. "But next time make sure your rope is not living." Cody grinned, "Yeah, for sure." They finally finished making a sturdy and strong but small raft. They even tied up some leftover reeds and branches to make a pair of oars! Soon they had pushed the boat into the river, jumped on and begun to sail down the Amazon River. They decided to take turns rowing. Cody and Lila volunteered to go first. As they were rowing, Cody asked Lila something, "Why are you shaking the boat so much?" "That's what I was going to ask you!" said Lila. They all looked down. To their horror, thrashing below them, snapping its jaw's, was a huge, black scaled Caiman, its amber eyes gleaming from the water! The three of them began to paddle like never before. They drenched themselves in water, but they did not care. The crocodile snapped off a part of the raft with its powerful jaws and if Cody hadn't been clinging on to Gary's t-shirt, he would have fallen in the river and drowned! Soon they managed to out-paddle the vicious Caiman and escape, thankfully, with all their limbs intact! "That was close!" gasped Gary spluttering water all over the raft. They made camp for the night by the river bank. Before they hit the sack they decided to fish in the river.

"I hear that you can find *Arapaima* in the Amazon!" exclaimed Cody, "They're one of the largest fish in the world!"

"Just as long as we don't meet any more caimans," chuckled Gary.

Mr. Geraldo had taught them about survival in the Amazon and his teachings stated that if one did not have food, one could fashion a net out of reeds and use it to fish in the Amazon. The three did exactly that but had their own strategy. Cody was to flash his phones torchlight and play his ringtone from one end of the river. The noises, bangs and bright light would make the fish swim away from him, to the other end, where Lila and Gary were waiting with a net in the water. This strategy worked for a while and they caught quite a few fish in the first and second rounds. But on the third round, nothing seemed to be coming near them.

"Do you think the fish have been scared off?" asked Lila.

Just then, ripples began to appear in the water.

"So many ripples!" said Gary, "This may be an Arapaima!" Cody flashed his torchlight and rang out his phone's ringtone. The ripple began moving toward the net. Then something went wrong. A sound was coming from their net. It sounded like a saw cutting into wood! Lila and Gary lifted up the net. They were in for a surprise. Small black coloured fish with red fins were chewing way at the net. Their eyes were small and yellow with black slits and their teeth were small but very sharp and powerful. Half the net was gone already. Fortunately Gary recognized these fish.

"Piranhas!" yelled Gary, "Drop the net!"

They let go of the net and ran to the bank, finally safe.

"But where's Cody?" asked Lila.

Cody was just standing in the river, but he was thrashing and trying to tug his leg out.

"What are you doing!" yelled Lila, "Get out of the river!"

"I'm stuck! There's seaweed around my leg!" said Cody, "And the Piranhas are swimming toward me!"

They grabbed Cody from both arms and tugged him out of the sand.

"You sure have a knack for getting in trouble!" said Lila.

"What?" complained Cody, "I don't even want to be here! I want to be playing Fortnite in my air conditioned room! Not getting chased by Piranhas in the Amazon river!"

The next day they set out again on the river and thankfully had an uneventful trip.

Soon they had reached a marshy bank with a path leading to a tree with a platform and lights coming from it! "She has a tree house!" said Cody, amazed.

"Yeah, I think so," said Lila grinning, "But not everyone can say they've sailed down the Amazon River, eh?"

"Nope," said Gary, he too was grinning. Who wouldn't be, after sailing down the largest river in the world! They trudged through the marsh path, their shoes making squelching noises as they hit the moist path. Cody was telling everyone jokes which Gary had to admit were terrible. "Why did the crocodile cross the road?" asked Cody, "To eat the chicken on the other side! Ha-ha!! What's orange and sounds like a parrot? A carrot! Ha-ha-ha-ha!"

Finally, after ten painful minutes of Cody's jokes, they arrived at the tree house. It was a huge tree with a thick trunk, algae and moss growing on it. They could not see the house as it was so high up the tree! But there was a rusty bell tied from an upper branch. Gary tapped the bell. It gave a loud clank and a ladder rolled down. They all climbed up the old, worn rope ladder and reached the house. It was a small house with clay potted plants on the window ledges. There were wind chimes hanging above the door, which gave off a musty smell. An old woman stood in front of them. She must have been around seventy or eighty years old because her face was quite wrinkled. She had white hair which must have been black when she was younger, as there were strands of black hair in the white. What was most strange about her though, were her beaded poncho and the tattoo she had on her arm, of a jaguar and a serpent! Serpents like the ones emblazoned on the ring, thought Gary.

She had a wheezy but kind voice. "Come in," she said smiling. She took them into a small room. There was a kerosene lamp on a shelf, burning faintly. There was a worn carpet on the floor and the smell of rain hung in the air.

"Are you Camila?" asked Gary.

"Why, yes I am! I am Camila Rodriguez, your great-Grandmother. Gareth, my boy! Don't tell me you didn't recognize me!"

CHAPTER FIVE

Gary's Great Grandmother

Gary was stunned. "She's your great-grand mammy Gary?" asked Cody surprised.

"I had no idea!" said Gary, thoroughly amazed. "I have a picture of your father who is my grandson, with you, right here!!" said Camila holding up a picture of a man with jet black hair and coffee brown skin, holding up a small, freckled boy, with flaming red hair, both of them were grinning at the photographer, who must have been Gary's mother.

"I never knew," said Gary amazed.

"But then, the Yanomami chief said that Camila was one of the last living Guarani!" stuttered Cody.

"I am!" said Camila.

"Then Gary, you're a descendant of the Guarani!" said Lila excitedly.

"Whoa," said Cody, "Can you do a rain dance bro?"

"I am a Guarani," said Camila, "though I definitely have never done a rain dance...but when I was around your age, I was sent to live in the City! I studied there and I got married there! But after my husband Pedro died and my son left home, I missed living in the forest. So I moved here! Your father was named after my husband, Pedro. He was a fine boy!"

That's when Gary remembered what he was here for. "Thanks Grandma, but my friends and I are trapped here! We have to find a stone of the Caipora or something," said Gary.

Camila's face went grim "You say you are here to find the Caipora?" asked Camila. "Then you are in great danger. I will tell you everything boy. A long time ago, the chief of our tribe, the Guarani, had a sacred stone. This stone held the spirit of the jungle, called the Caipora! It was a huge beast with the body of the mighty jaguar and the tail of the sly serpent! It served only the chief and protected the jungle. That's why the emblem of the Guarani was the Caipora," said Camila, rolling up her sleeve and showing them the tattoo. "When the chief became old, he decided to keep the Caipora in a stone. It was a beautiful green emerald." "Like this?" asked Lila, holding up the ring.

"Yes," hissed Gary's great-grandmother. "That ring has a terrible history. I will tell you about it later. The chief placed the Caipora in a statue, a statue of the Caipora itself. He hoped that it would still protect the jungle. But he was wrong. The Caipora cannot, because of the terrible crime of a greedy man. One day, a man by the name Phineas Geraldo Santos was in the forest. He found the Caipora, locked in the statue. He was a greedy and evil man. He was the type of man who whips animals for amusement and chops trees when he felt angry. He definitely didn't care if he stole the spirit of the jungle from the forest. I doubt he even knew the Caipora resided in the stone! But even for him, prying such a huge stone from the rock was an impossible feat for one man. So he chipped of a part of the stone and placed it in a Guarani ring. In fact, that very ring is the one you're holding now Lila! He fled that night, as the Guarani would not take to it kindly that he had stolen part of their sacred stone! But there was a prophecy. It said that a century hence from then, the last descendant of the Guarani would return to the forest. He or she would unite the ring with the true stone and the Caipora would protect the jungle once more! And that person who is meant to do this, is you Gareth." "So, that's why Fernandez said that we could return home only once we re-united the ring and the stone!" said Lila, now excited. "Do you know Fernandez?" asked Gary.

"No, I'm afraid I don't know anyone in the Amazon called Fernandez, my boy!" replied Camila "But you must, certainly be very tired. Why don't the three of you sleep here tonight? It is not safe to put up tents at the river bank in the night. The crocodiles in the Amazon hunt during that time and will devour any unsuspecting animal or person on the bank!"

Gary and his friends, not wishing to meet anymore crocodiles decided to lodge at Camila's tree house. She led them to a small wooden table on which she placed three bowls of what Gary recognized as (ugh) succotash! He managed to choke down the succotash so as to not hurt his great grandmother's feelings. Cody however was having a silent laughing fit watching Gary eat it. After dinner, Camila laid three mattresses for them to sleep on. As they slept, Gary thought about what Camila had said to him, while watching the full moon through the open window, as the sound of chirping Cicada's filled the air. Was he really a descendant of the Guarani? Was he destined to unite the Caipora? With these thoughts Gary drifted off into sleep full of dreams involving Cody and Lila with Jaguar heads and Fernandez turning into the Caipora.

The next day Gary woke up to the cawing of macaws. Cody, Lila and Camila were up too and once again, it seemed that the macaw's had taken a liking to Lila because of her hair. He knew this as Lila's hair once again was full of 'surprises'! They ate breakfast and drank some hot 'Cacao' (Camila had picked the beans herself); she also corrected them that the beans were Cacao and not 'Cocoa' as the Europeans had started calling it. They soon were ready to leave. Camila marked the location of the shrine of the Caipora on their map, so they knew exactly where they were headed. They said their goodbye's and headed to their destination. They came across many types of insects and birds, which thankfully (according to Lila) were not interested in her hair. They came across a clear, sparkling lake, with beautiful white flower shrubs growing nearby. There wereanimal's drinking water at the lake, thankfully not predators. There were Tapir's, Capybaras and many more creatures. "We don't have such beautiful places in the city, mhm," said Cody breathing in the flower scented air. Lila had gone to stroke the lustrous black fur of a tapir, but it snorted water on her from its small trunk like nose. She didn't seem to like the animal very much after that.

Cody was having a look at a strange type of Amphibian that was white in colour and had red feathery gills!

"What's that?"asked Cody.

"That's an Axolotl salamander," answered Lila, "Camila told me that these salamanders were smuggled by Phineas Santos and his men to the Amazon from Mexico. That's their real home. They're not meant to be here.

Gary noticed a strange type of flower growing on the bank. It was yellow in colour and gave off a strange smell. Gary and his friends drew closer. "I wonder what that is?"

asked Gary. Suddenly, he felt really dizzy. He could not see his friends. The scenery around him seemed to change! He was waist deep in a strange kind of substance. It smelled familiar too. Though not in a good way. He then realized this liquid was succotash!!! Huge figures, rather like Oscar award trophies, rose out of the goop. "Eat Succotash!!!" chanted the figures, "It's delicious!" "No!!!" screamed Gary. "I've had enough of it!!!" It was truly a nightmare. Just then a hand caught him and jerked him backwards. "No!!!" yelled Gary. "Don't make me!! Don't make me eat it!" He started screaming out in Portuguese, "Eu Odeio isso!!! É nojento!!!"

"Who made you eat succotash?" asked a voice.

"Cody?" asked Gary. "Oh thank goodness! I started hallucinating about...wait how did you know what I was hallucinating about?"

"We guessed," said Cody, raising his eyebrows.

"Oh it was horrible!" exclaimed Gary,"Oh why couldn't I hallucinate about Tamales instead?"

Then he thought of something. He swallowed nervously.

"Uh...you guys didn't see the *whole* thing unfold did you?"

"Yeah, we know," chuckled Lila, "we watched you sobbing and screaming in terror. You should be ashamed of yourself. A Brazilian descendant of Guarani begging to eat Mexican food."

"Oh," said Gary, feeling rather embarrassed, "And anyway succotash isn't an indigenous food either...I think the hallucination had something to do with those plants!"

"Yup," said Cody, "I wish we could bring one back for Giller. He'd love it."

Gary and Lila laughed along with him. Soon, after one more day of hiking in the jungle, they arrived at a huge temple, with mossy stone walls. There were carvings of jaguars, serpents and other snarling beasts emblazoned on the wall. There were also carvings of what had to be Gods, with feathered helmets and weapons shooting arks of fire. Cody seemed to be a bit afraid of these wall carvings. There were two rusty levers on either side of the door. Cody and Gary pulled them hard and the gates of the temple opened. Inside was an open courtyard. The ground was paved with stone. Carved on the side walls were jaguar heads. "These Guarani must really love their jaguars," muttered Cody. He was just about to take a step when Lila shouted, "Don't!"

"Why?" Cody asked bewildered.

"Bet you anything that that those jaguars shoot poison darts!" said Lila, "Watch."

She threw a pencil from her bag to the floor. Sure enough, a dart shot from the jaguar so fast, it pierced the pencil! She picked up the dart carefully.

"This has got to be the Curare poison. It canparalyse you and kill you!" said Lila.

"That doesn't sound like a lot of fun," whimpered Cody.

"I have a plan though," Said Lila, We can throw our stationary from school onto the floor, so the pressure plated areas are revealed to us!"

So they threw their pencils and rulers onto the floor and soon enough almost all the squares on the floor were littered with stationary. The three of them tip toed across the floor, careful not to step on the areas with a pencil or ruler on it. They finally made it across!

"Whew, that was close!" said Gary sweating. They had now arrived at a large stone door. There were vines and moss growing all over it. Together the three of them pushed open the door. Inside, it was musty and damp; the floor had a thick layer of dust. It was completely dark and Gary could not make out anything. Suddenly an ear-splitting howl filled the air. It was so loud that Cody jumped about two feet in the air, a feat he could have never done under normal circumstances. That's when Gary noticed that they were indeed not alone in the chamber. Sitting on the ledges above them were howler monkeys, shrieking and howling at them, their shrieks echoing in the chamber, making them sound ten times louder! That's when they started pelting them with banana peels, fruit seeds and nuts. Lila brought out her umbrella and shielded them from the rotten fruit. Gary felt, that umbrella had helped them so much during the trip, one could write a book about it, "The Adventures of Lila's umbrella!" The umbrella was now worn out and torn and it probably wouldn't be of much use now on a rainy day. "We have to make a run for it!" shouted Lila. "This umbrella won't last much longer!" The three of them ran for the door opposite them. They pushed it open and ran out. They were finally safe. Lila pulled a banana peel from her hair.

"Who knew that howler monkeys could be so dangerous!" grumbled Lila.

"They would make great basketball players, though!" said Gary.

"Yeah!" said Cody, "Maybe after we get out of here we could start up a basketball team of howler monkeys! I can see the headlines, 'the Portuguese primates'!"

Lila grumbled something that distinctly sounded like 'boys". That's when they acknowledged their surroundings. They were in another courtyard. But this one was different. There was a huge pool like structure in this one. The water was a murky, green colour. Joining the stone on either side of the water was a thin stone column. But on the other side of the water was a huge statue of what looked like a serpent with a parrot's head and beak! Its tongue was protruding which made it look much scarier. "Mbói Tu'ĩ!" gasped Gary. "I know this legend, my father told me about it. In Guarani mythology there are seven legendary monsters. They were t'sukalu, Mo'nai, Luison, Ao Ao, Jasy Jatere and Teju Jagua. But the most powerful of all was MbóiTu'ĩ. He was the guardian of aquatic and amphibious creatures and also lord of water! He was also considered the most dangerous...which is not good for us, as we have just come across a huge statue of him."

"How do you even know this stuff?" asked Cody, his mouth hanging open in awe.

"Then there's probably something swimming in that water below!" said Lila, "I hope it's not crocodiles!"

"No," replied Cody, "something tells me it's going to be way worse than a crocodile."

"We have to go across," said Gary confidently, "Do you want to go back home or stay in this 'nightmare on earth'?" The three of them inched across the column over the water. Cody went first. Then went Lila. Then it was Gary's turn. Suddenly when he was halfway across the water, something huge, scaly and slimy slid out of the water, splashing Gary. He could not see it, but it lashed out its tail and whacked the column. Gary tumbled off the smashing Column and fell into the depths of the murky water.

All Gary could make out were the two shapes of Cody and Lila diving in. He had taken swimming lessons with them that summer, so they wouldn't drown. That's when he saw what actually resided in the depths of the pool. It was the most horrifying thing Gary had ever seen. It was about seven feet long. It had arms at the front, but none at the back! Its eyes gleamed yellow. Instead of teeth however it had a pair of huge, sharp fangs. Seaweed shaped fins protruded from its back; its skin was pearly white. It lashed out at Gary, slashing with its fangs! Cody, Lila and Gary began to try to swim out, but one of its fangs caught Gary by the back of his pants! It tried to drag Gary in! But Cody and Lila pulled him from the fang as hard as they could. Then everything went black.

When Gary opened his eyes, he wasn't in the pool anymore. He was on the opposite bank! He spluttered out a lot of water and looked up. Cody and Lila were leaning over him. "Are you alright?" asked Lila a tone of panic in her voice. "Yeah," replied Gary. He stood up. He was standing in front of the statue of Mbói Tu'ĩ. The left part of his pants had been torn from the bottom.

"Whew, that monster was scary!" said Gary with a sigh. They approached the statue. A carving was written on it. Apparently Camila had given Lila a translation book of the Guarani language Tupi! Soon she had deciphered the code. "It says that this is something with a lid but it's not a container, it's something with a socket but it's not a plug. What do you think it is?" asked Lila.

"I think it sounds like an eye!" said Gary.

"Then maybe there's something in the statues eye that can get us out of here!" said Cody.

Lila began to climb up the statue and finally reached the eye. "There's nothing up here!" yelled Lila.

"Try twisting it or something!" yelled Cody.

Lila did it and suddenly, the statue began to tremble! Lila jumped and they all stepped back. The statue had split into two and a passage was leading them into another chamber! They stepped forward. It was a dead end with another inscription on it. Lila translated once again. It said, "This animal can be quite long but it doesn't have great height. It can have deadly venom though, so beware its bite."

"What do you think it is? There are plenty of animals in this rainforest that are venomous!" said Lila.

"Let's just look around the other inscriptions and see if there's anything depicting a poisonous creature," said Gary. They searched the whole chamber until Cody gave a shriek of delight.

"Look a serpent!" said Cody excitedly, pointing at a rather sinister looking carving of a cobra. They pressed it and the chamber parted, opening into another room. This one had the inscription, "Five lettered I am now, but this does remain to be seen.If I wasn't under you now, you'd be falling with screams and shouts."

"That has to be the floor. We'd be falling alright if it weren't for the floor," said Cody. They placed their hands on the floor. The second door opened. The next chamber's inscription read, "Put my words together and you'll see, everything's just not a dream. Final challenge you have reached. Do it and just wait you'll see."

"Hmm...if we put the riddles together, It spells 'snake floor', but in English that would be 'snakes on or in the floor'," said Lila. Then suddenly, part of the floor opened. A huge Anaconda slid out of it!

"Uh...Lila, I think we realize what the riddle means," stuttered Cody. "The riddle isn't just a riddle. It's real!"

Gary stared frightened at the Anaconda. "That thing can crush you to pulp!" muttered Lila. "Guys stay still. If we don't make a move it might leave us alone."

"'Might leave us, isn't very reassuring," muttered Gary. The three of them stood as still as statues. The Anaconda slid around them and flicked its tongue back and forth. Gary knew why it was doing this, as they had studied in biology that snakes smell using tongues, not their noses! It slid across Lila's shoes and finally, it decided that the three of them weren't its prey. Gary couldn't believe that the serpent had decided to leave them! And that's when Cody decided that now was a good time to sneeze. The Anaconda turned around in seconds and slashed at them with its tail. They jumped to safety but the tail had made a big crack in the floor, opening a deep chasm. The snake lashed out at them once more and this time Lila fell into the chasm.

"Lila, no!!" yelled Gary and Cody. They rushed to the edge of the chasm. She was hanging on to the crumbly rock with both her hands. The two of them heaved her up just as the rock crumbled from beneath. The door of the chamber cracked open and the whole room seemed to be crumbling. The three of them rushed outside just as a huge rock fell on the Anaconda.

They had arrived at a courtyard. It was huge and had stone walls surrounding it. In the centre was the statue of a jaguar with a serpent entwined around its neck, but it seemed to emerge from the animals back like a tail. In the serpents mouth was a huge, green emerald, glinting in the sun! "That's got to be the stone of the Caipora!" said Cody excitedly. "We can go home! Also why does the Jaguar have a snake protruding from its butt?"

"I don't know," answered Gary, "but we have to unite the ring and the stone now!" That's when a rather familiar deep, silky voice rang out "Well, well so you've got the emerald!" And there before them stood two men wearing sneers on their faces, who Gary recognized as Colonel Fernandez and Mr. Reginald Geraldo, their history teacher.

CHAPTER SIX

The Caipora Returns

"What are you two doing here!" asked Gary bewildered.

"He wants to know why we're here!" mimicked Geraldo, "What do you think we want boy! Pretty tropical flowers? We want the stone!"

"But why?" asked Lila, "It's not of any importance to you!"

"Oh, do you even know how you got here?" said Geraldo, "I taught your class about the rainforest so you'd know everything about this place! I had the ring, which I placed for you to pick up in the cafeteria! I arranged with Fernandez to pick you up and take you to his house and tell you everything! I had him follow the two of you during your whole trip, to make sure you made it here! Three children can't survive the Amazon on their own! Except of course those certain times, when Fernandez couldn't interfere and help you, like when you got yourselves captured by the Yanomami and had to fight that crocodile. You weren't supposed to meet the old woman though."

Gary was shocked. Geraldo and Fernandez had tricked them! "And now you want to know why I want the stone, boy? Well, it's for revenge! My ancestor was killed when he came back for this very stone by a monster that the Guarani chief had placed here. He died trying to get the stone from which he had taken a piece and set in a ring! Yes, my boy! I'm the great-great-great- Grandson of Phineas Geraldo Santos!" said Geraldo. Now Gary knew why Phineas Santos sounded familiar! His middle name was Geraldo! And now, I've come to take what is mine! I will be rich! Stinking Rich!" said Geraldo laughing.

"Remember that we share the treasure, Geraldo!" said Fernandez, "After all, I did a lot too and also supplied the Mercenaries and henchmen!"

Fernandez snapped his finger. At least seven men in camo-pants and t-shirts came forward. They were all very muscular and held assault rifles. Two men stood guard next to Gary, Cody and Lila to make sure they didn't escape.

"You can't take the stone!" yelled Cody, "It's impossible for one man!"

"For one man? Yes," jeered Geraldo gesturing to the henchmen, "but I have plenty!"

Five henchmen approached the statue with heavy crowbars. After about five minutes, they had prised the emerald from the serpent's mouth. Suddenly a bluish-green light began to glow and the whole temple began to tremble, rocks began to fall and the three of them ran to take cover! A huge invisible force wave spread from the statue. The trio were knocked off their feet and Geraldo was flung backwards, the emerald slipped from his hands. He soared over the crumbling walls and from over them, the huge beastGary had been attacked by, erupted from the water and snapped up Geraldo.

Well it was nice knowing him, smirked Gary.

Many of the henchmen were crushed by rocks and only three remained, all surrounding Fernandez. That's when the statue cracked open, glowing green and blue light emitting from the cracks. A huge beast stepped out with gleaming blue fur and green and black rosettes. From the huge Jaguars back emerged an emerald green serpent, its tongue flickering in and out, hissing at them. A pair of scarlet and gold Macaw wings protruded from the beast's back. The Caipora was free!

The huge beast circled them, licking its gleaming white teeth with a pink tongue. The Caipora lunged at Fernandez and his henchmen. With one horrifying gulp, it swallowed two henchmen. Then it stared at the emerald on the floor and began to approach it.

"No!" screamed Fernandez. "That emeralds mine, now that Geraldo's dead! I'll be rich for life!!!"

The Caipora lashed out with its paws and knocked him aside. As if by magic, thick ropes began to bind themselves around Fernandez. Gary grabbed the emerald and offered it to the Caipora along with the ring. The Caipora stared at him long and hard. Then the ring and emerald seemed to bind together and disappeared in a flash of green light. The Caipora's eyes began to glow green. It gave them a nod of approval and flew away into the jungle.

"Arghh... get them Jango!" yelled Fernandez addressing the last henchman.

But before he could approach them, someone yelled "Stop!" They all turned around. There before them stood Camila, surrounded by what looked like the whole Yanomami tribe! Two warriors caught hold of Fernandez and the others proceeded to capture his henchman. "How did you find us?" asked Cody.

"Oh, Lila asked me to come here if you weren't back in three days," replied Camila, "she's a smart girl. And what happened here?"

Gary told her everything, about how Fernandez and Geraldo were traitors and the Caipora. "So it does exist?" asked Camila in awe. "Wish I could have seen it."

The Yanomami had tied up the Colonel and his henchman Jango. Apparently the Yanomami had arrived with Camila by boat. The trio arrived at the banks of the Amazon and saw the huge Yanomami wooden boat, painted in beautiful patterns. They sailed all the way to the Yanomami village. Camila's house was nearby but she decided to accompany them to the village. Soon they had reached the village by nightfall. There were some forest guards waiting to take away Fernandez.

"This is no Colonel Abraxo Fernandez!" said one of the forest guards. "This is Ridgewell Gonzales, the famous gun smuggler! He has been shipping stolen goods and weapons along the Gulf of Mexico!" Soon the guards took him away. The Yanomami prepared their traditional dish of mushroom and jungle fowl wrapped in corn bread to celebrate. Gary soon discovered that it tasted exactly like Tamales! After dinner, the three friends sat together on a rock in the village. The Yanomami were playing music with drums, flutes and reed pipes. The sun was setting and the sky was golden with a pink hue. Gary was feeling relaxed and full. The Cicadas werechirping once more, the tropical night birds were singing and the frogs were croaking in the night air.

"So, we're finally going home!" said Lila grinning, "That was quite an adventure, wasn't it? I can't wait to meet our parents though."

"Yeah, me too," said Gary who was feeling a little homesick.

"Yeah, about that…," said Cody, "what exactly are we going to tell our parents, when they ask us where we've been?"

"They're never going to believe us," said Gary. "But I can't wait to meet them. Also, we're going to arrive in style by a Brazilian military helicopter!"

"Yeah, awesome!" said Lila, "But the school doesn't have

a history teacher now. What are they going to say, 'Oh, your history teacher happens to be a descendant of an evil treasure hunter and he was eaten by an amphibious monster in the Amazon rainforest!'"

"Yup, something like that," said Cody, chuckling. Suddenly a macaw flew over Lila and dropped 'something' on her. "Stupid @#*&%$ Macaws!" grumbled Lila. The others started laughing and then Lila too joined in.

"That's the Caipora's way of saying thanks," said Gary grinning.

CHAPTER SEVEN

Home Sweet Home

It had been six months since Gary and his friends had gone on their adventure in the jungle. Gary rushed out of his house to catch the bus to school. He went to his usual seat at the back with the Corcovado's.

"Hey Gary!" said Cody grinning, holding up his I-phone, "Remember that adventure of ours? Well guess what? Someone wants to make a book about it!"

"That's fantastic!" said Gary.

"I know right!" said Cody, "Who knows we may be even put in a movie! 'The Quest for the Caipora'! They may even make us super muscular and stuff. I want the movie rights if that happens!"

"Sure," grinned Gary.

Soon after school, they were walking through the hallway when a familiar voice rang out.

"Hey look, Its Rodriguez the weirdo!" mocked Giller, "Want another knuckle sandwich?" Gary turned around and gave Giller a punch on the nose with a sickening crack. Giller recoiled holding his bleeding nose.

"Next time Thomson, pick on someone 'your'own size, because trying to bully people bigger than you is just begging for a punch on the nose!" said Gary grinning.

"So the Amazon toughened you up?" asked Lila. She too

was smiling widely.

"Yeah, I think so," said Gary, "Cody says someone wants to write a book about our adventure!"

"Really?" asked Lila. Yes, someone did write a book about their adventures! The three of them told him all about it. He wrote it and decided to publish it. You may be wondering where you can buy that book. Well you just finished reading it.

Author's Note

When Gary punched Giller, he was not in fact, 'toughened up' by his Amazon adventure! He simply felt confident about it, as he had faced worse than 'Giller the Griller' on his journey. If we too feel confident about things, we can accomplish the impossible!

Brazil Fact File

National animal: Jaguar
National bird: Toucan
Capital: Brasilia
National sport: Football
National food: Feijoda (type of meat stew)
National anthem: Hino Nactional Brasiliero
National language: Portugese
Popular Cities: Rio de Janireo, Salvador, Manaus, Sao paulo
What it's known for: Christ the Redeemer, Amazon rainforest, Samba dance, football and coffee

Tamale Recipe

Gary's favourite food is Tamales! Well guess what? You can make it too, with this simple recipe!

Ingredients:

Readymade tortilla (Available in most grocery stores) - 6 of them to serve 12

3 pounds of chicken, with skin removed and shredded

1 cup shredded mozzarella or cheddar cheese

½ cup of frozen peas

½ cup of stuffed green olives, sliced into halves

2 cups of salsa

2 cups of self rising cornmeal mix

Process:

1. Stir chicken, peas, olives, cornmeal, salsa and cheese in bowl.
2. Heat up the tortilla and spread it out.
3. Place the mix of ingredients in the tortilla.
4. Roll up tortilla over filling.
5. Wrap it in corn husks
6. Add 1-inch of water to deep pot with tight lid. Arrange the tamales upright in the container. Boil it over medium-heat flame for 25 minutes.
7. Remove the tamales from steamer and let them stand for few minutes. Then remove corn husks.
8. Enjoy your tamales!

Interesting Facts About The Amazon

- The rainforest is called the Amazon because it is located along the Amazon River basin.
- The Amazon is often called the "lungs of the planet" because it produces about 20% of the world's oxygen!
- The Amazon forest occupies about 2.2 million sq. miles. It is 9 times larger than the state of Texas!
- One in ten known species on earth dwell in the Amazon rainforest. It includes 40 thousand species of flora, 430 species of mammals and 300 – reptiles, as well as a large number of insects (butterflies just over 1,800 species)!
- The number of birds that live in the Amazon rainforest accounts for one third of the total number of bird species on earth. The most famous symbol of the forest is a Toucan.
- It is also important to mention the human population of the Amazon. The Rainforest is home to nearly 3 million indigenous Amazonians. These indigenous people represent about 300 tribes, and they speak in 170 different languages!
- The Amazon rainforest is depleting! Recently there was a forest fire in the Amazon rainforest that lasted 16 days!
- Annually, the Amazon forest gets over 95 inches (240 cm) of rain. About 50% of that recycles back into the atmosphere through evaporation.
- The number of species of fish that live in the region exceeds the number of species of fish that's found in the whole territory of Europe! Amazon also is home to the world's largest fish – Arapaima. Their length reaches

an impressive 8.5 ft. (2.5 m in length), and they have a record weight of 552 lbs. (250 kg)!

- If you decide to travel here...remember you are at the risk of being attacked by a Puma, Jaguar or Anaconda...and don't worry about acid squirting spiders...they don't exist!
- The rainforest gets dust for its soil from the Sahara desert, which is located on the other side of the Atlantic Ocean! An estimated 50 million tonnes of dust from the Sahara is naturally blown into the Amazon forest, coming all the way across the Atlantic Ocean. That's really amazing!
- The first settlers inhabited the Amazon about 11,200 years ago.

Glossary

Ao Ao – the Guarani deity of mountains and hills. He's often depicted as a sheep with fangs.

Brazil – The largest country in South America

Caipora – The Guarani protector of the Jungle. It is depicted as a man with red hair on a wild boar or a jaguar with macaw wings and a snake tail. It is often confused with Curupira, another forest spirit, known to have feet pointing backwards.

Guarani – A South American tribe

M'boi Tui – A Guaraní deity of water and aquatic creatures. He's often depicted as a serpent with the head of a parrot.

T'su Kalu -The Guaraní deity of fire. He resembles a giant.

Tamales – A Mexican dish of tortilla wrapped around steamed meat.

Knuckle sandwich – Slang for a punch on the face.

Amazon River – the largest river in the world.

Luison – The Guarani god of death and everything related to it. It is depicted as a dog merged with an ape.

Mo'nai- The Guarani deity of open fields. He is depicted as a serpent with two colourful horns.

Ethnography – The study of theculture of various tribes.

Teju Jagua - Guarani god of caves and fruit. He is depicted as a lizard with seven dog heads and eyes that shoot fire.

Tupi – Language of the Guarani tribe.

Arapaima – Among the largest freshwater fish in the world

Ao Ao – the Guarani deity of mountains and hills. He's often depicted as a sheep with fangs.

Caipora – The Guarani protector of the Jungle. It is depicted as a man with red hair on a wild boar or a jaguar with macaw wings and a snake tail. It is often confused with Curupira, another forest spirit, known to have feet pointing backwards.

Guarani – A South American tribe

M'boi Tui – A Guaraní deity of water and aquatic creatures. He's often depicted as a serpent with the head of a parrot.

T'su Kalu -The Guaraní deity of fire. He resembles a giant.

Tamales – A Mexican dish of tortilla wrapped around steamed meat.

Knuckle sandwich – Slang for a punch on the face.

Amazon River – the largest river in the world.

Luison – The Guarani god of death and everything related to it. It is depicted as a dog merged with an ape.

Mo'nai- The Guarani deity of open fields. He is depicted as a serpent with two colourful horns.

Ethnography – The study of theculture of various tribes.

Teju Jagua - Guarani god of caves and fruit. He is depicted as a lizard with seven dog heads and eyes that shoot fire.

Tupi – Language of the Guarani tribe.

Arapaima – Among the largest freshwater fish in the world

About The Author

Rian Nair is a 13-year old boy who currently lives in Chennai, India. He is a dreamer as well as a history buff. He is a student of Sishya School and is currently in ninth grade. He is writing other books that will soon be published.